Waiting to Sing

A Richard Jackson Book

story by Howard Kaplan

Waiting to Sing

illustrated by Hervé Blondon

DK
Ink

DORLING KINDERSLEY PUBLISHING, INC.

A Richard Jackson Book

Dorling Kindersley Publishing, Inc.
95 Madison Avenue
New York, New York 10016

Visit us on the World Wide Web at http://www.dk.com

Dorling Kindersley books are available at special discounts for bulk purchases for sales
promotions or premiums. Special editions, including personalized covers, excerpts of
existing guides, and corporate imprints can be created in large quantities for specific needs.
For more information, contact Special Markets Dept., Dorling Kindersley Publishing, Inc.,
95 Madison Avenue, New York, New York 10016; fax: (800) 600-9098.

Library of Congress Cataloging-in-Publication Data
Kaplan, Howard, 1950-
Waiting to sing / Howard Kaplan; illustrations by Hervé Blondon.—1st ed.
p. cm.
"A Richard Jackson book."
Summary: A family that loves music and spends many hours at the piano
is devastated by the death of the mother, but those still living find consolation
in the beautiful music that also remains.
ISBN 0-7894-2615-3
[1. Piano–Fiction. 2. Music–Fiction. 3. Death–Fiction. 4. Mother and child–Fiction.]
I. Blondon, Hervé, ill. II. Title. PZ7.K12898 Wai 2000 [E]–dc21 99-041081

The illustrations were created with pastel.
The text of this book is set in 17 point Garamond.
Printed and bound in U.S.A.
First Edition, 2000
2 4 6 8 10 9 7 5 3 1

For my father
—H.K.

In the memory of
Bernard Girodroux
—H.B.

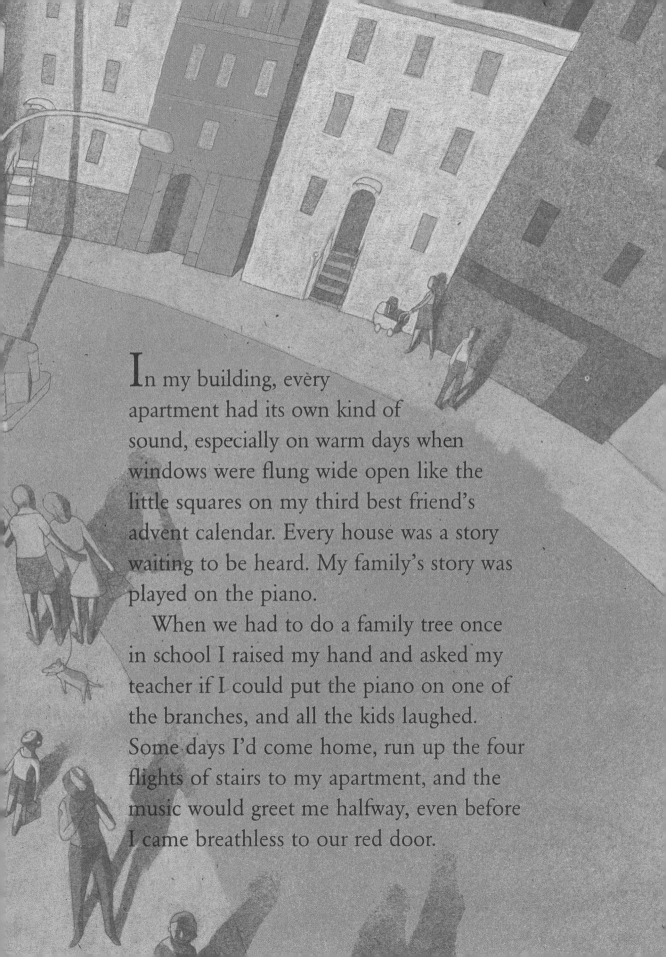

In my building, every apartment had its own kind of sound, especially on warm days when windows were flung wide open like the little squares on my third best friend's advent calendar. Every house was a story waiting to be heard. My family's story was played on the piano.

When we had to do a family tree once in school I raised my hand and asked my teacher if I could put the piano on one of the branches, and all the kids laughed. Some days I'd come home, run up the four flights of stairs to my apartment, and the music would greet me halfway, even before I came breathless to our red door.

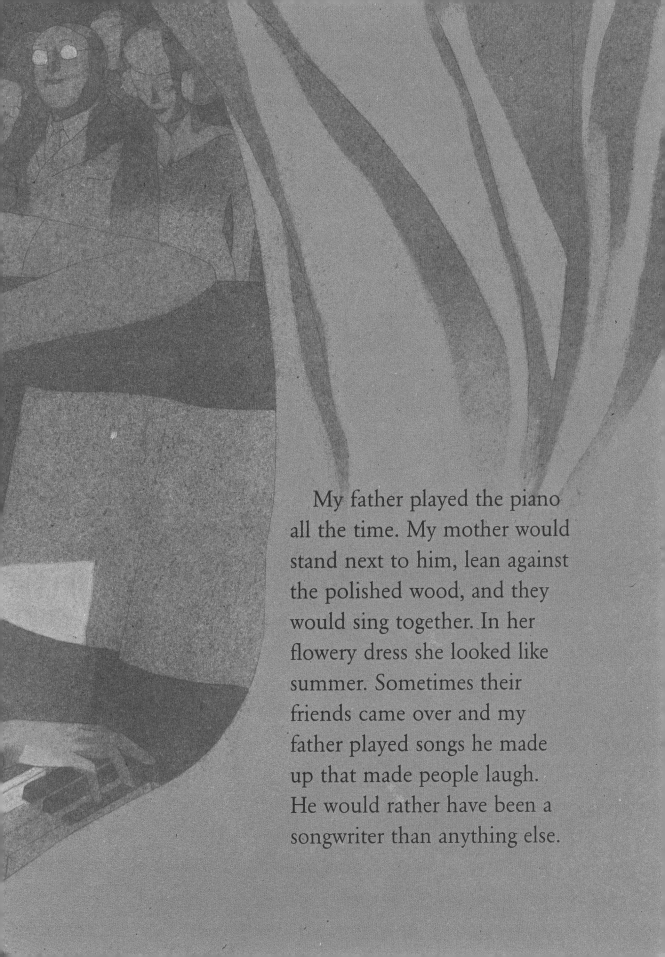

My father played the piano all the time. My mother would stand next to him, lean against the polished wood, and they would sing together. In her flowery dress she looked like summer. Sometimes their friends came over and my father played songs he made up that made people laugh. He would rather have been a songwriter than anything else.

If he played at
night when I was going to sleep,
I'd keep my bedroom door open
just the right amount so I could
hear the music faintly. It covered
me gently, like the whisper of
an August blanket.

When he finished, he'd fill my favorite green glass with water, and hold it for me while I sat up in bed and took a few sips. Then he'd tuck me in for the night. The glass stayed on the windowsill collecting moonlight till morning.

Even before I was old enough to take
lessons, my father taught me how to play
the piano. I'd sit next to him on the
wooden bench that was filled with sheet
music. It was a hidden library that
none of my friends knew about.

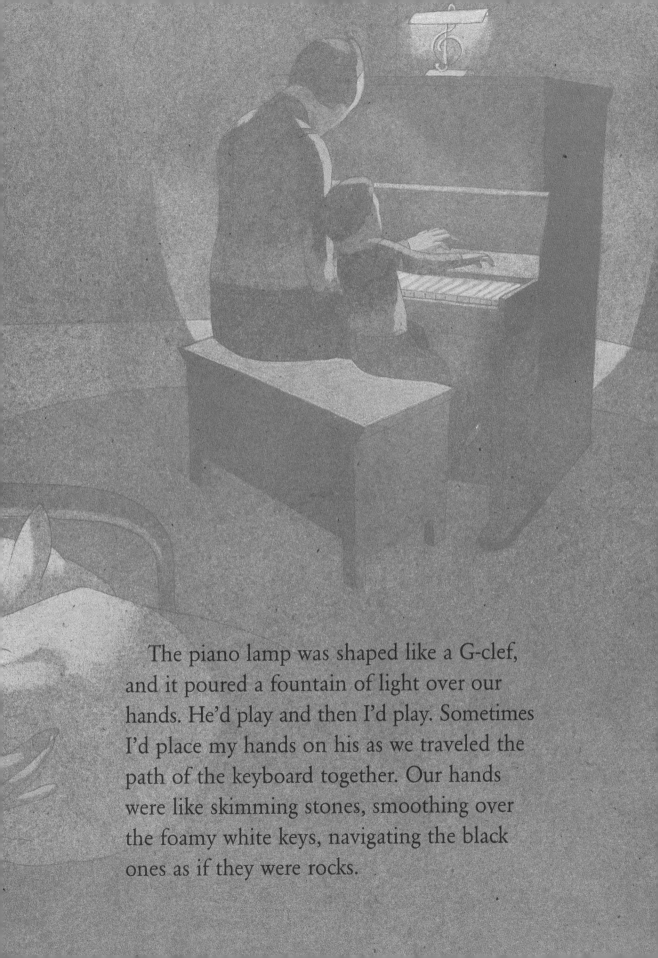

The piano lamp was shaped like a G-clef, and it poured a fountain of light over our hands. He'd play and then I'd play. Sometimes I'd place my hands on his as we traveled the path of the keyboard together. Our hands were like skimming stones, smoothing over the foamy white keys, navigating the black ones as if they were rocks.

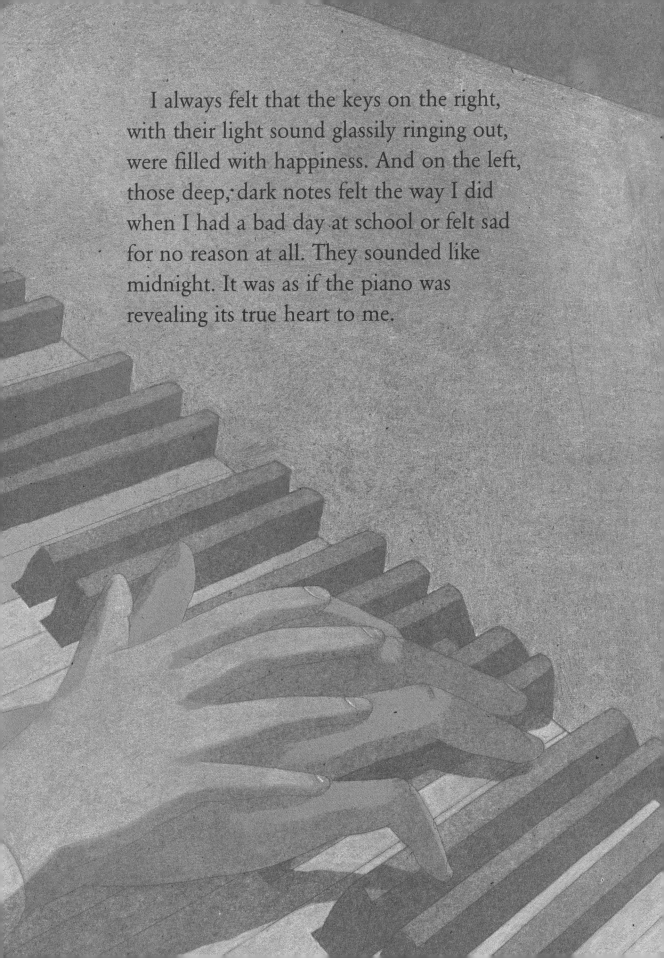

I always felt that the keys on the right, with their light sound glassily ringing out, were filled with happiness. And on the left, those deep, dark notes felt the way I did when I had a bad day at school or felt sad for no reason at all. They sounded like midnight. It was as if the piano was revealing its true heart to me.

When I was a bit older, my father and I sat down together and he took out a piece of music my sister learned to play by heart before she went off to school, "Für Elise" by Beethoven. Once my father smoothed open the music, the notes looked like a thousand birds had landed in front of us.

Later, I tried to count all the notes, but I gave up at seven-hundred-forty-four because I still had to do the left hand! There were notes everywhere, peeking over and below the margins I was used to.

My father placed his hands over mine and we began to play.

I took lessons with my sister's teacher, who came over every Tuesday afternoon for an hour. If I practiced hard enough, I'd be in the fall recital. I played best when I turned out all the lights except the piano lamp, and practiced under its generous white moon.

During the week I'd practice after school, though I'd complain about it to my mother, who was always on the lookout for wrong notes, even when she wasn't feeling well herself.

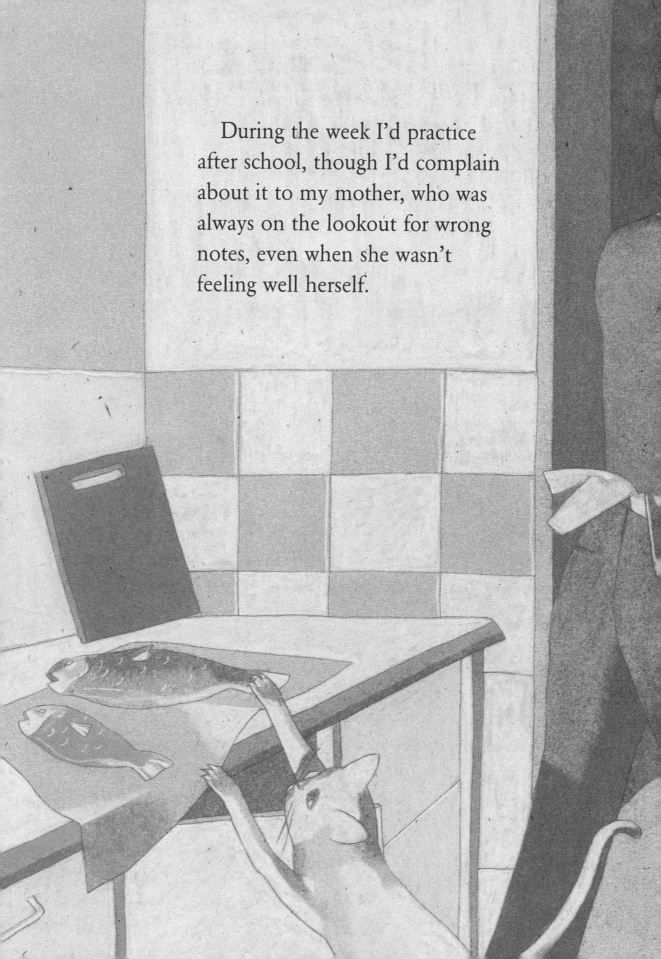

If I hit too many, she'd
come out of the kitchen where she
was preparing dinner, and she'd
stand behind me till I got it right.

One summer we spent a week on Cape Cod, but my sister stayed behind, saying she was too old for a family trip. We took long walks along the sand collecting beach glass—blue was my favorite. I even helped an elderly couple dig for clams. Each one I pulled out of the shallow water was like a secret. If it was small enough to pass through a metal ring you had to throw it back. Mother loved everything about the sea: how it changed colors in the shifting light and left the taste of salt on our skin. The tide made our footprints disappear behind us.

When we returned home and Mother
began to get sick, "Für Elise" is what she
liked to hear. I'd send the music around
the corner and down the long foyer to her
bedroom where she rested. I loved her by
heart, but one late summer evening she
passed through the ring of the world
and died.

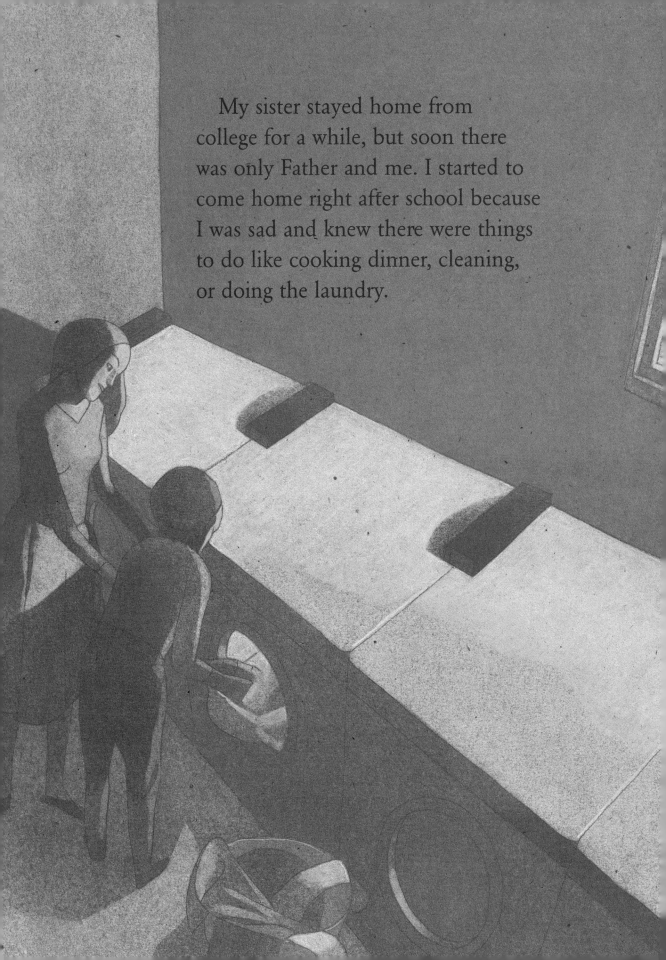

My sister stayed home from college for a while, but soon there was only Father and me. I started to come home right after school because I was sad and knew there were things to do like cooking dinner, cleaning, or doing the laundry.

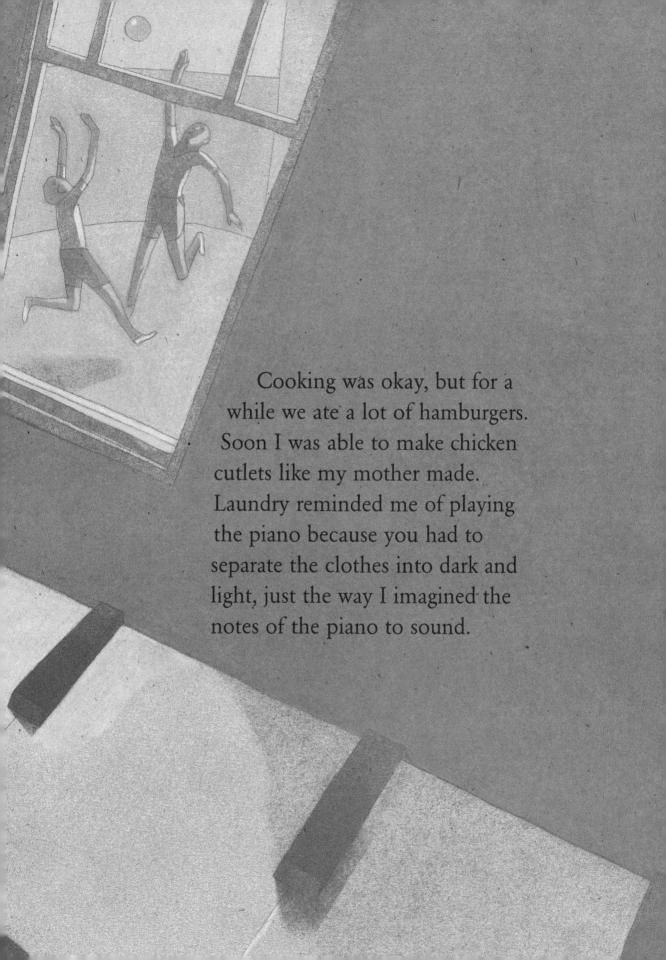

Cooking was okay, but for a
while we ate a lot of hamburgers.
Soon I was able to make chicken
cutlets like my mother made.
Laundry reminded me of playing
the piano because you had to
separate the clothes into dark and
light, just the way I imagined the
notes of the piano to sound.

I tried to play the piano, but it wasn't the same. And when I played wrong notes I looked to the doorway where she once stood, but it was empty. I looked behind me, but no one was there. It was like pressing a doorbell when no one was home. Everything went quiet for a time. We closed the piano. It seemed even the G-clef lamp ran out of light.

Some days I'd look out the window and watch my friends with their mothers and families, and I'd turn away before they could see me. I missed my mother tucking in my school shirts or trying to slick back my hair with a wet comb, even though it had bothered me at the time. I missed the blue beach glass of her eyes. Outside, the sparrows were leaving the September trees, looking for a home elsewhere. The cool, gray sky looked the way I felt inside.

My father and I didn't say much to each other. He stayed in his room and I stayed in mine. He stopped making up songs, and none of my parents' friends came over to laugh anymore. No more birds landed on the piano.

One evening I sat at my desk and heard music from the dark part of the house. The first notes seemed so familiar, E and D sharp, like two friends calling out to each other. My father was playing "Für Elise." It had such a pull on me, it made me think of the bread dropped in a fairy tale when you're finally ready to turn around and leave the woods.

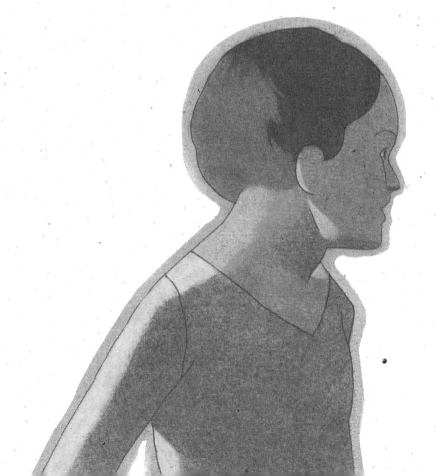

I walked from my bedroom to the piano
bench, as if holding on to the music for
balance, and sat by my father's side. But we
didn't say anything. We didn't have to. We
let the piano speak for us. It was our way of
crying, the way it had once been our way
of laughing.

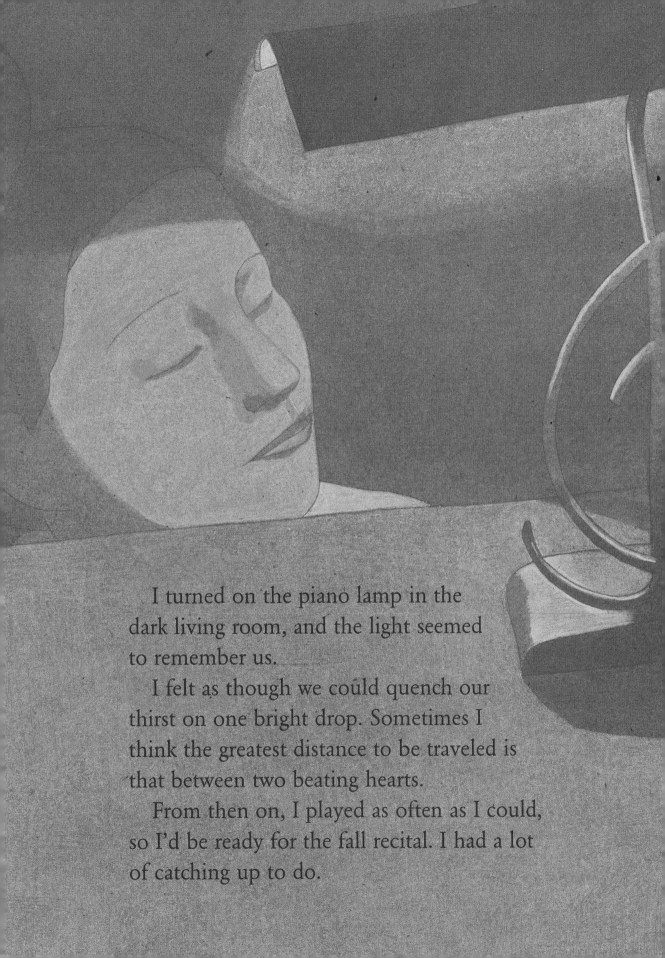

I turned on the piano lamp in the
dark living room, and the light seemed
to remember us.

I felt as though we could quench our
thirst on one bright drop. Sometimes I
think the greatest distance to be traveled is
that between two beating hearts.

From then on, I played as often as I could,
so I'd be ready for the fall recital. I had a lot
of catching up to do.

A few weeks later, it was time.
My sister came back from school for
the recital and sat by my father in the
first row, an empty seat between them.
I tucked my shirt in for the hundredth
time and ran my fingers through my
hair like a comb.

When it was my turn to play, I stood to the side of the piano, then bowed to the small audience. I sat down, and when I opened the sheet music, my thousand birds were waiting to sing.

afterword

Beethoven wrote "Für Elise" for a woman he loved. Her name was Therese, but between Beethoven's poor handwriting and the use of splotchy ink, his early biographers couldn't make out her name clearly and thought he had written Elise. He finished "Für Elise" on April 27, 1810, and presented Therese with his copy of the score, known as the autograph, the following month. It has been missing ever since she died.

Though he was in love with Therese, it seems she did not have the same feelings for him. In his letter, he quotes the great German poet Goethe:

> *People are united not only when they are*
>   *together*
> *even the distant one,*
> *the absent one is present with us.*